CW01559160

GAIUS IS

PART I

There was only the art of perception when it came to what was noticed at the sight of those persistent night-clouds. Dark purple could be seen, but so could black, and if the eyes stared just enough for the darkness to settle, small bursts of blue could be noticed, blue that made it out of daylight and snuck through the pores of the sky into the sunless mouth of midnight. He wanted colours, whether they were above him, below him, or around him; a colourless environment could do very little for him; to be among colour was to feel real, to feel that living had a beat, a rhythm. It had always been that way. His mood was daring and he was walking and he could feel the profundity of things as he moved through the swells of evening, approaching the night that was harbouring something unheard of, and he knew it because it felt like no other night, and no other mind could convince him otherwise. The evening was rich, a time to seek hidden doors and sail through them as if on the other side existed a magnified experience. And it was with the counting of those trees to his left that he embarked on a passage, a quiet one, quiet because its meaning had not yet formed, its words were silent, but he was stridently aware of it. Instantly the world was no longer a cave of mediocrities, where the sky was a dome to restrict the freedom of sight, where the wind blew to send the leaves asunder, the birds chirped to disturb, the sun rose only to penetrate the sleeping ignorance of departed gazes. He had not seen the world in this way for some time, and what was it, he pondered, what exactly was it that had been the thing to unclog such a firm perception, to pull the lever that sent him up and out of the sticky state glued to him only in the hour before? It was only in the hour before that he had poured hot candle wax over the coffee stain on the windowsill as a small protest against its ugliness, that he had huffed with disdain at the blanket placed incorrectly on the sofa, that he had walked out into the fading day and saw nothing but phantom-bodies with indefinite outlines and poisoned smiles, all around. But what had happened? And why was the transition so quick and so obscure? Why was it such a mystery that he could perhaps cry at the enchantment of the sky whereas it would have taken a thunderous pressure to force out a single tear in the hour before? A lilt of wind took his eyes to the golden street lamps. Each steel post held three lanterns, like a Cerberus, ablaze with honey and fire. Drawn by their light, he trailed inwards, into where the town fostered beating life, soon arriving at a street on which he had never stepped foot. There were smokers by the stainless doors of restaurants, flaunting their breaths, small dogs scurried along the curb as miniature clumps of shadows, trancelike music and howling chants were thrown off balconies above, someone shouted "hallelujah" from a speeding car— but all of these things, every single one of them was a component to a picture of multidimensional adventure. He truly had not felt this way for a long while, so connected to the signs and pulses and movements around him, and he set free a sigh with a faint chuckle to the sky as he took his hands out from his pockets and made his way through the shapes and sounds, a bustling auditorium that was life. The wind seeped through every space, carrying along a piece of a newspaper, and it flapped and fluttered chaotically like a bird gone haywire. Glued to the journey of the page, his eyes followed it in distorted circles until it crashed into the wooden leg of a table, flapping as it failed to get past. And then a boot, a shiny black boot on a bobbing foot caught his attention and led his gaze up the curve of embroidered denim and the fluff of a coat up to a pair of eyes that were lost to the current of a deep thought. So far away they were, in a chasm that belonged to some other realm. The brown and the roundness and depth of them seemed to contain a familiarity. He had seen these eyes before, he thought, and when they fell back into the moment and slid upwards to meet his own, he realised, right away, that he had known these eyes, deeply, and they him.

— Theodore?

Her voice came out with a stutter and a surprise, but at the end of the word was a bend of sincerity, a buzz of joy that matched a recognisable smile and the soft raising of brows.

— Yvonne, is that you?

— Yes—yes! Oh, Theo, I can't believe this.

Theodore scooted under the awning and Yvonne sprung to her feet and the two of them shared a tight embrace, a hug that contained a familiar scent through which the gracious punch of memories lurched—dim and in rippling fragments, but thumping loudly to the forefront. They sat facing one another, their hands on the table, almost touching. A trumpet horn on a passing bike honked. Gossiping words of a distant conversation briefly snatched the moment. A whiff of heat blew over them from the opening door of the restaurant, and when it settled, the air became frozen, and the entirety of it was fused with recaptured memories, gently forming into an enhanced picture that they could retreat into their minds to admire before returning to the unexpected instant.

— Yvonne, you won't believe this, but I was just—I—

Here, he realised that he could not find the words to carry what he wished to say. He wanted to tell her about this sudden rush that had just oozed through him and lit him up, this sense that he was approaching something new and untold, without the foresight to what it was and when it would appear. And then, as he began to find the tips of words, he changed his mind; he wouldn't go into it, for perhaps she would get the wrong impression, or he would fail to make her understand. For what did it matter anyway? He shook away the thought and spoke:

— Sorry, I'm just so delighted to run into you like this. You know, I've never gone down this lane before, and tonight I did for some strange reason, I don't know why, I wasn't going anyway in particular, I was just kind of walking, strolling, and to see you here—oh, it's just great to see you.

Some tender thing inside of him had awoken as he spoke these words; it was akin to the blossoming of a flower while the stem rose through his body and the petals came out through his mouth, for he spoke with warmth, a warmth that had been missing for some time. Yvonne sighed a smiling breath.

— You live around here now? she asked.

— I live down that way, he said, pointing his finger towards the east. I've been here for half a year now. Have we been neighbours the whole time?

— No, no. Actually, I've just moved in. Right above us.

She tilted her head as if pointing upwards with her nose, then lay her elbows on the table and her face in her sprouting hands, her eyes lit with a small contemplation and a penetrating enigma that Theodore recognised right away.

— Right up there?

He looked up to an open window on the floor above.

— Right up there. I came down here for a quick break. I arrived yesterday morning and I'm still in the middle of unpacking.

— Am I disrupting you? he asked, his eyes widening. I can come to see you another time.

— Oh, I'd love nothing more than to talk with you right now. Do you want to come up? We'll be surrounded by boxes, but I have a sofa, and tea, plenty of tea.

He blinked into a pause, before speaking:

— Yes, let's go.

At the top of the florid staircase, Yvonne turned the stiff key and opened the door to a wide room of cream walls, on one of them a tapestry of patterns like the veins of sliced fruit. Rows and piles of cardboard boxes were scattered here and there. With her feet, she pushed some of them to the side and fell onto the sofa, the springs sighing with her. It seemed that the night was building itself upon a peculiar sense of freshness, of expansiveness, and it grew through and billowed out from Theodore's chest, synchronised with his heartbeat, not fast, nor slow, but rather in the middle, the fine epicentre, from where he could move like a breeze without the slow swing of lethargy or the haste of a tempting tempest. He was calm, almost meditative, and in such a fine state he went and sat beside her, letting his limbs sink into the sensation of static being.

— Why have we been worlds apart, Theo?

She was leaning on the arm of the sofa, staring right at him with eyes that illuminated their chosen subject, like a lighthouse sending its shaft to the rocks on the shore, obscured by a dark hour. She leant forward.

— Your hair, it's lighter, isn't it? And it's gone all curled under the ears, hasn't it? It looks even lovelier than I remember it. Although I've always admired the waves in your hair.

Her words were airy and joyful. He blushed lightly, then he looked up to the freckled ceiling. A silence intruded, one that did not contain the edges of reason, made out of air and the particles of thought that fly through it. And as the two of them sat there in this speechless instant, Theodore watched glitters of memories pass, before turning to face her.

— What do you make of things now? he asked.

— Things?

— Well, I guess—life. And everything that comes along with it.

— Now how can I answer a question like that without musing on everything, on living in its entirety, without us going on till morning? she said, laughing. Let me think, what do I make of things? I'll start by saying this: things are a lot easier now, than they used to be.

— Really? How so?

— Well, for one, I feel like I can talk now, Theo, really talk and stand before what I'm saying. It's like my thoughts come out in large wedges as opposed to the soft, broken crumbs they used to be. And what's more, I love listening to others. I know I've always been quite the listener, but I realised that often I would only half-listen before, that I could rarely truly grasp what others had to say because I wasn't completely letting things in, you know?

He looked into her eyes which were ripe with feeling.

— The last time we saw each other, Theo, I was so preoccupied with what I thought was approaching, what I assumed I'd become, that I wasn't really noticing the things that were there around me. It's strange, the me I used to be, she was so often unaware, so focussed on what not yet was, on the things she couldn't see. I was often quite vacant, rootless.

— That's a harsh way of thinking about it, no?

— But it's true. Everything is different now. Things aren't so muddy anymore. I used to have this fear that I'd grow up, move to another city, and at some point in my small life, that sly expiration of joy, of curiosity, would creep up on me and I'd be left with nothing to hold onto other than the past. So I'd try to get ahead of things before they got to me. But, you see, all of that went away.

As she spoke, Theodore looked towards a jewel-like sparkle from a ring refracting on the mantelpiece—so alive, it gleamed. It was like a sign that the edge of an unfathomable reason had come to greet him. A reason for what? He was unsure. It was a light, little in size, specked with a shimmer of something more real than even himself, to halt the journey of a roving eye and keep it frozen as if fracturing the procession of time, with every vivid feature one could foretell emblazoned along its curves. He listened to Yvonne meander along her thoughts aloud, and so swept into her words he was, and as she went on to tell the tales that came so effortlessly to her, not even the clock that ticked above their heads could have persuaded them to exit the illusion of timelessness. For they were now, in all senses, beneath the sway of symbiotic words. And on and on they went, forgetting the night, forgetting obligations, away from the interminable hum of the world.

— So, said Theodore some moments later in the night, the lights were so bright that I could barely see anything other than orbs and beams through the squint of my eyes. It was me sitting before them all, the cello between my legs. I was coming to the end of the sonata, my eyes closed, my feet planted into the floor, like this, my knees on the edge of a quake. Then, something shifted. I felt like I had forgotten.

— Forgotten what?

— I don't really know. Expectation? Limitation? The feeling of incapacity? Maybe it was all of those things, I can't seem to pinpoint it exactly, but whatever it was, it was no longer there. I had wandered into a stream, without volition it seemed. And that final note, the note that somehow brought out an influx of many more, the note that should have been cast by a fleeting stroke, came from something wonderful, and whole. I had conjured it somehow, and I'm not even sure anyone else heard it the way I felt it, the falling curtains refused me even a glimpse of the faces before me. But what I had felt, that's what stayed with me long after that night. It was in the playing of that final part, while the stick in my hand drawled into a cry, that I had become more than I previously had been. It felt like my hands could somehow paint anything into the air, that my mind was the property of nothing. In that moment I belonged nowhere in particular, but I was so embraced. Five, six, seven seconds. It could have been more. After the curtains closed I dropped the stick onto the floor. I could no longer hold it.

— Why not?

— I couldn't bear the thought of having gone so long without it, that very thing that had constructed what came out at the end of the sonata, the fact that it had been hindered for so long. And once again it was gone, it had left me. So it was almost easier to pretend that it had never arrived, that I had imagined it, that it was a mirage, for how could it have been so foreign to me and why had it only shown itself then? And why did it vanish so immediately?

As the kettle squealed in the kitchen, he stared at the floor and began laughing.

— Maybe I'm not making any sense.

Yvonne stepped out for a moment, and then returned with two steaming mugs she placed on the oak table before them.

— It's difficult to comprehend, this kind of thing, right? Sometimes attempting to define can only be done by embracing the narrowing walls of words. I think I understand this sort of thing to be like an instant of inspiration, free and untampered. You said that it felt like a forgetting, right? Maybe in that moment you didn't gain anything, and instead, momentarily, you lost something that was keeping you from it. I don't know what you felt, Theo, but I think it's easy to forget what we are capable of, to be so oblivious to the things our minds can really hold, to keep ourselves held back from those things.

He felt comforted as he listened to her, at the fact of being heard, of another mind so engaged with the heart of his experience. He had always known her to be a torch to senses, encouraging the expansion of those around her, attempting to illuminate details they could often not recognise alone. And here, nothing had changed. He spoke:

— You know, sometimes I find myself lost in a daze, a sense that I'm almost sleepwalking, and I try to think my way out of it, or I attempt to get past it with the knowledge of being here, being conscious, and that often leads me to spiral into questions I cannot find an answer to.

— Such as what?

— Such as: Am I being less than myself? And, if I am, how can I be more?

But suddenly he was shaken out of the heavy question as the shadow of a cat's tail drew a bend along the wall in front.

— It's fine, Yvonne assured him, this little one snuck in the minute I got here. She keeps crawling in through the balcony, coming in and out of the window as she pleases. I don't know where she belongs, but I like her being here.

— I think she feels at home with you, he said, his eyes chasing the shadow's fluidity.

Then the cat pranced through the air, and as it made it to the top of a small tower of boxes its swift body leapt from a falling box that tumbled to the floor along with cotton stems and sheets of golden brocade. Yvonne stood and ran to the box, delicately placing it back upright and then removing the tape.

— That could have been a lot worse, she said, exhaling.

She pulled out and inspected oddly shaped structures that held the form reminiscent of human figures. And then another, and another, their shapes blanketed by piles of shadows.

— What are those things?

— These are my sculptures. I started playing around with clay last winter. I made one of these and then I couldn't stop.

Theodore stood up, and halted.

— Can I take a look?

As he approached, the almost-silent murmur of mystery was painting itself through the ears of his mind, like a distant nebula that is found nowhere. He watched her vision skim along the limb of a figure, assiduously, and then pinch the head, making sure it was intact. Aligned with the angulation of a pointed finger, her eyes marked themselves along the expanse, the curves, the lines.

— Here, she said, passing him a sculpture.

It stood upon a small base of wood, one foot firmly planted, the other facing upwards, bent at a perfect angle at the knee. The arms were sprawled outwards, a ballerina pressed in motion, the hands etched with the outlines of fingers. From the waist to the shoulders, the figure twirled moderately like the subtle bending of a creek. He held the head up to his own, meeting small, imperceptible features of faces like those in the bark of a tree when shadows of sunlight are made. In the solid manoeuvres of the clay he found a puzzling appearance, falling through him like a sudden, silent revelation, prodding him, calmly, urgently. But he wasn't sure how to bring it to cognition, nor was he even certain it was truly real. It fluttered like a reverie, and it tore through the pores of his memory so he could see through the imagined eyes of all his prior selves. And in that immeasurable venture, that plunge into the faint touch of impossible, what came was a mesmerism, a kiss of awe at everything known, perceived, at all that could be found. He trembled in stillness.

— How did you make this?

— It's pretty intuitive, said Yvonne. It starts off small and then it evolves with time, with thought, and persistence. If you'd like you could make one yourself. I have all the material here with me.

From another box, she pulled out an armature of aluminium wire affixed to a small, circular base of wood.

— This is the skeletal structure. I made it yesterday. You build and mould the clay around it, and then you work your way along each part of the figure, in whichever way you feel.

She opened a bucket of wet clay, took out a small clod and placed it into his hand.

— Start with this.

In his palm, the clay was moist, round, purposeful. Holding onto it, its unseen purpose like a harbinger of delicate urges, he looked down at it and perceived it as if it were the foremost word of a story, the primary piece of something that would become—become what? And like the mouth of a hungry animal reaching to a tree for sustenance, he placed the clod onto the face of the armature, pressing down firmly until it wouldn't let go. Then he pushed gently around the edges until it was hugging it, a part of it, the first flesh of a newborn mind that would soon be held by a body.

— That's it... Keep going.

But when he looked inside the bucket, at the swarming mound of clay, something startled him, for he felt his heartbeat expand and his pores become moist. What was before him seemed to be of the greatest importance, seemed to contain endless knowledge. It was the clay of eternal potential, unseen, but so imaginable and so endless, too vast to fathom, too vast for his meagre hands that were sweating with unworthiness.

— Maybe another time, he said, looking away.

— If it's time you're worried about, you know you can stay here as long as you like, right?

— It's not that. I'm afraid to start it, that it will consume me.

— Oh, I understand. It's a big task. Maybe some more tea?

— Yes, more tea would be nice.

Under the abundant night, they talked, and shared heaps of laughter. Every so often, Theodore noticed his gaze steer towards the bucket of clay, as though inside were an undeniable mystery, beating and roving and pounding.

And then, somewhere between an ignited memory and the sporadic imitation of sounds outside the window, he forgot about it altogether.

Some moments later, after talking spiritedly for hours, Theodore was sitting on a stool by the window, Yvonne was lying on the couch, her eyes half-closed, listening to his mind stream along curls of thought.

— The steepness was making me nervous, but I knew I couldn't look up or my hands would tremble and I'd have to let go. I knew that if I fell, it would be fine, the instructor would gently guide me back to my position and I'd begin again. At one point I froze, and I had to close my eyes and whisper myself out of the spell so I could keep going. Strangely, I didn't fall, and I surprised myself when I made it to the top. It was a blip of the mind that I needed to adjust in order to get there. And, oh my, it was exhilarating to be up there, but it was the feeling that took place in the seconds before I decided to take the final leap that was indescribable.

Yvonne hummed a sound that suggested the imagining of a vivid scene. As an air of sleepiness crawled in, a minute or two of easeful silence passed, and then she spoke:

— Theo, do you think I'm going to like living here, in this city?

— I think you will. At least, I think you'll find pieces of home here. I certainly have.

— That's nice to hear. Recently I've been out of place with where I've been. I've gotten used to home feeling like a distant dream. And I've been having a hard time forming bonds with others, I've felt that most people have little time for the things I deem most important, like this. It's why I've been wanting to get out and find something that feels right, where I can integrate and feel a sure sense of home. It's why I've come here. But this morning, I woke up confused and frightened that I was making the wrong decision. I had packed my bags, boxed all of my belongings, but when it came to it I almost didn't let myself go. But seeing you has confirmed something for me. I get the feeling now that being here will be a really good thing.

She paused, laughed slightly, then turned to him.

— I know I'll get to it all eventually, but there's so much I want to tell you now.

Her words were moving slower, drifting into a mist.

— I want to hear everything.

He placed his finger on the window and wiped away a small white dot that was a splat of paint. Beside the thin layer of wind that made it under the gap in the window, a feather-like brush of clarity came upon him. And as he looked at the spotless night outside, a sigh exerted from him like an airy melody. It came from the sense of a hush and sway within, like soundless, untouched waters, and along with it came the silent spring of unfettered thoughts, so alive and so open to flux and caprice.

— You know, he said quietly as he looked at a swaying leaf barely hanging onto the stem, at times I think of myself standing against the backdrop of the world, and everything becomes solid, opaque, and my mind—it becomes this scanty, tender thing blowing in endless winds. And sometimes, in these moments, whether I wish to find my feet or simply let it all wash over me, simply existing overwhelms me.

He took a sip of tea and let silence return, before turning to see Yvonne under the rise and fall of restful breaths. As he captured the smile of her pupils sliding into a dream, he remembered days, a handful of years ago, on which they would wander between their dorm, cafés, woodlands, the library, and the echoic lecture hall in which they sat most days and acclimatised to the history and philosophy of art, how they watched birds fly over rooftops and spires, talked through fanatic moods, sang wistfully by the pond, read passages from books beneath all kinds of skies, cycled along concrete neighbourhoods, stole wishful coins from fountains when they needed money, in the mornings watched films on a box television, and in the evenings adored tree-filled views from bridges while they discussed anything in wonder and humour. He chuckled as the breeze blew the memory away, then let his hands meet the cold window.

— When this feeling arises, if I let it take over me, every direction I turn to is one of infinite paths, colours seem almost supernatural, memories seem so entwined with the feeling of here and now, breathing is like floating in mystery. Forms somewhat lose their description and become these illusory curves that say nothing other than patterns and outlines. It's like a dream seeping into being. I can only be still; movement would require understanding, and I have none.

He kept watching the leaf, and then, as the seconds passed, he noticed the wind move away from it and the leaf return to stillness, like the immediate halt before the final breath of a dance.

— But sometimes, he whispered, that's the place you need to be, I think, to get further. Isn't it?

And immediately he wanted to write it all down, what he just spoke, whether he would somehow remember it word for word or just the foundation of it, for it had come out of that rare state when the integuments of the conscious mind are lifted, and perhaps it would help him in the future. So he looked around for a pen and a piece of paper, then made his way to the table, fixing his eyes on the clutter.

What happened next happened with so much impetus, he only had to let the thought come over him for a split-second for it to move him: he opened the bucket and stuck his fingers into the clay, like roots expanding headlong into loam. He noticed his heart beating at a tempo that implored him to stop, and he didn't know why but he also felt that urge for discovery come through like the pound of a hammer, and when he lifted his hand, stuck to the touch of his fingers was a remnant of the fine clay. He studied it as if he were holding a rare bird. It was like an element of pre-consciousness, like the unsung substance that formed the work of his childhood imagination: the snow before the snowman, the grains before the sandcastle, the sticks and leaves before the garden den that soon befriended the sun and the wind-blown moths and butterflies, and at night, the stars. He felt that on his fingers was the embryo of a future escapade, and that if he were to tread through, something, whether its appearance would take the epithet of large or small, would become. It would come to be realised. All he needed to do was to let his hands be hands, and his mind play through them. And when he pinched a piece of clay and placed it onto the armature, connecting it to the other piece, he knew he wouldn't stop. Each little bit called for another. Slowly, the tea light candles on the shelf lost their spark, and outside he heard a distant waltz twinkling like dots of a harmless fire. But he was so focussed, so keen and so persistent, and he wouldn't cease until the entire armature was covered in clay.

It happened sooner than he imagined. The process was quite like biting into an apple, how the first bite seems the most important, but then through the succession of bites, tearing away at the flesh becomes more and more natural, until the action becomes an almost subconscious pleasure, one bite after the next until you are left with only the peduncle and the seeds. As he held the clay-covered body in his hands, its posture carrying the hope of half-fledged entirety, he sensed a shiver brush against the back of his head, kissing the tips of his hair, and he thought: I will hold dear this small thing like it is a spark that has fallen from the sun. He looked around the room. The curtains were restful, and through them shone the residue of a distant sulphur-yellow light from a street lamp—blinking, blinking, blinking. The light illuminated the silhouettes of boxes by the window, pulsing shadows of wraithlike architecture, and in front, the pretty magnolia on the table, and beside everything, Yvonne's rising and falling breaths.

Next, he began adding more clay in various quantities to the different parts of the figure, incrementally, his focus snatched by the movements of his fingers and the placement of each piece. As he massaged his thumbs over the shoulders, pushing inwards the sides of the neck, he briefly realised that he had not felt so tethered to the tail of instinct like this for a long while, so distant from the patterns of calculation that, if he were to intellectualise, would have destroyed this feeling by digging towards the centre of its pulse—but he had to cut off the realisation of it almost immediately, so as not to break the spell of intuition. The clay had consumed him; every thought that did not pertain to the clay had no place in his mind, the kind of thoughts that blink into existence and then fly away like crumbs being blown from a table, disseminating into nothing. He was caught in the motion, the act of there to there, taking from the bucket and giving to the figure, taking and giving, taking and giving. It was like moulding wisdom into small acts of change, his pinch the beak of a bird that constructs a nest, viscerally. He liked the way it felt to slide his fingers across the clay, to press down and watch each singular part become a part of the oneness he was conjuring.

Soon, he had added and distributed enough clay for it to resemble the essence he had in his mind. It stood upon the base now with a posture reminiscent of so many he had seen before. He studied the left arm—immediately a thought told him to bend it at the elbow and raise upwards the semi-formed hand. So he did. Then he took a step back, then another, to see it as one. He could still hear Yvonne breathing, and he tried not to wake her with a chuckle at the happenings of this night that had crystallised into a fortunate discovery. He looked between the curtains at the outside that was wreathed in night, and he felt that he was a protégé of the now plentiful darkness, the darkness who had promised the discovery of what was vague and confounding. In an elusive manner, there was something about the night, it was almost like, in stinging whispers, it was chanting: unravel me. Then, looking again at the figure as it stood proudly in the bare light, without a second of prudence, his fingers began to tend to the edges of the clay, working from the feet up, the tips and the nails moving in gentle glides and pushes to add flicks and strokes of the subtlest texture. There wasn't any time for analysis, only intuition, and it was an intuition that had not an ounce of self-doubt, that resounded, without a question, through the hallway of thought, the sound of beatitude. When he arrived at the face, with the play of his fingers and a soft pressure, he made two dents for eyes, and pinched, with tiny contortions, the appearance of a nose, a mouth, and at last, ears. Then with the touch of nails on his little fingers, he added flicks to represent the curls of hair. And while exhaling a breath of satisfaction, he leant back and observed with studious admiration. Here, despite the lack of resemblance, he saw it as if it were a microcosm of himself, as if in nurturing it, he would be nurturing himself, in painting a mind for it, he would be enlivening his own, in holding it gently, gently, he would be holding himself.

After cleaning up the mess and then placing a soft robe over Yvonne—it was all he could find amidst the boxes—he quietly headed out, watchful over the sculpture in his hands, aware that any sporadic movement would perhaps disfigure it. Stepping out onto the pavement, headlights running across his vision and a vague drizzle falling through the air, he held the sculpture up so he could inspect it in the blinking light of the streetlamp. He couldn't recall the last time he had been so fond of a material thing. Such a puzzling sensation it was, but he didn't examine it, for the staggering enigma of it could not live inside the state of awe he was in; he sensed, tentatively, that to try to get to the kernel of it would be like attempting to think a way out of thought itself.

He walked home, holding the base, careful to keep the sculpture suspended in the air, his other hand holding an umbrella so not a single drop of rain would touch it. He observed the way it stood, the way it was so unknowingly sure, and at the same time contained an irresistibility like no other thing he had held.

At home, he placed it on the kitchen table among scattered belongings. Staring at its intricacies, he removed a tiny bit of clay from a shoulder and placed it onto an ankle, thickening it just slightly. Now it could stand with the certainty of balance. He gazed, deciding that it was complete. He imagined it breathing, that oozing through was a fluid that indicated a life: blood, or perhaps it was more like sap, or instead a fluid unlike anything there was, with a word unutterable by the human tongue. And fixed in the head, as tiny and supple as it may have been, lived a seed of thoughts, curious, sentient, capable of self-preservation.

— What are you and why are you suddenly so vital to me? he whispered.

As he gave it the tenderness of his eyes, he couldn't pluck from his mind the idea of a name—to compose a name from nothing at all, to catch hold of the fleeting sweep of a word as it soars by and assign it to this now complete form. His eyes wandered along things in the room: the mulberry tiles, the cranberry chocolate on the counter, the twirling leaves on the windowsill, the hanging mirror, the patterned mosaics above the door. He whispered words, names, sounds, invented phrases that came to mind, but nothing landed with the thump of certainty. He looked at the things on the table: toppled books, tubes of oil paint, semi-filled porcelain mugs, and a vase of chrysanthemum. Chrysanthemum? he thought, rolling his eyes amusingly. Then he noticed, to his side, the unfinished newspaper crossword he had left that morning. He placed it before him and focussed, sticking his eyes onto the letters in those tiny squares, thinking that none of them would suffice. Then his circling fingers led him to the letter G, the letter of a word that began a new, incomplete word. He checked the clue.

— Forename of Julius Caesar, he read.

It was there in his mind, somewhere beneath the folds of recognition, and if he were to focus on pulling it out, it would come. And soon it did. He remembered it and immediately wrote it down: Gaius.

— So that is it? he whispered to himself. That is the name?

Something about the name and the sound of it lingered in time when he looked at the sculpture. Something about it was like the threads of intangible serendipity. And it was the sweetest feeling, to hit the middle mark in the spot of exactitude. That was the name. The name was Gaius.

PART II

When Theodore was a child he tripped over a rock and grazed his chin along the concrete ground. He watched his blood, spit and tears form a concoction of his sudden agony, a substance he had never seen. Lifting his hands from the ground, he noticed the dots of red coming through the skin of his palms, pins upon pins of the sharpest sting he had known. Forcibly, a wail of release came up from the abyss of his stomach and out through his mouth that was dripping incessantly. Tears fell onto his scratched lips, salting the ache and the sting. He had not once experienced a gush of blood in this way, he hadn't known it to be so relentless and wet. Shock had grasped his bones and yet he was unaware of it, and when he stood on his feet the distant trees were wobbling and the sky became a swarm of speckles, sending thousands of shooting arrows all around. His cry was muffled and distant, like the call of a baby whale separated by depths of ocean. He had to let the rush of severity pass before he was able to, with small steps, make his way back home, where, at the door, he cried to his worried parents through squinting eyes. They took him in and cleaned him up, tending to his cuts. As they washed the blood from his mouth he stood over the sink and stared at it fusing with the running water, thinking that each drip seemed like a pellet flying into a rushing river and evaporating into puffs of smoke, swirling into red hysteria. He succumbed to a trembling halt while he thought about blood, his blood, leaving his body with no resistance, without a shred of his own doing. He couldn't believe how so much of it could be dispelled from his mouth so easily, sent away to a dark and forgotten place.

Later, when he sat in front of the mirror and examined his cuts and bruises, he thought about the loss of blood once more. He imagined himself with open wounds, two unstoppable gashes across the soles of his feet, dispelling blood like an uncontrollable leak of rain from a ceiling, the blood reddening the floorboards beneath him, his heart losing the momentum to keep on. He pictured his body as the final drops left him, emptying him, and he imagined that he would turn expressionless and pallid, almost paper-white, his arms would limp like melted rubber, and his eyes would be two white holes at the beginning of an endless wormhole to nothing. He would be a bloodless sack that was once a child. He wondered if he would die, without blood, or if life would hold on to what it had left of his poor, useless body. Suddenly he thought that he now knew more about death than he had known in his seven years of life. But Theodore had never seen anyone die, nor did he ever wish to. To him, death had always been a foggy thought. As he stared at the imaginary puddle of blood in which he sat, despite the uncertainty of it, he supposed then and there that the act of dying would be similar to falling asleep. But to sleep forever would be a terrible thing, he pondered, he would go insane if he were to be banished to the space between dreams and forced to remain there forever. One time he had overheard somewhere the idea of heaven, of an afterlife in which he'd soar and have the entire galaxy at his fingertips, all the pleasures he wished for at a call, but he thought now that if it were to be true, he would certainly no longer be himself, and if he were, then it would be nothing but a trick, an optical illusion. As his mother walked into the room, he came out from his daydream and, with muffled words, asked her what will happen to him after he dies, uncertain she would have any clue herself. She fell into immediate defence, a serrated clench in the line of her jaw, telling him not to imagine such things, that he was too young to think about a thing like that. When she left the room and he turned back to face the mirror, he was pricked all over by a needle-like shudder and a small palpitation in his heart, and suddenly he quite liked the thought of the continuation of life after death. He remembered a time he had seen a painting of a human-angel hybrid above the mantlepiece in his grandmother's country home, the wings plumed and gilded, the hair wild and untamed as leaves of autumn. He had asked his grandmother what the fascinating creature was, and she told him that it was the form of human life after death: an ethereal, god-like being with wings so fierce and a spirit so mighty. At the time he quietly rejected this hypothesis, but now, as he imagined it once again with all of its blinding boldness, quietly in his mind, he told himself that at the moment of his death he would instantaneously wake up as this being that resembled something from a folkloric tale, and this being would live unendingly. And so he would get to live forever.

Once the dread departed, he painted details onto this narrative of his, inventing a world in which an assemblage of creatures roamed, each with their own otherworldly characteristics. He shared this revelation with some of his friends at school, and quickly the idea started getting around, swimming through the curiosity of his fellow pupils, until one day, on the subject of a deceased scientist in class, one of them brought it up with the teacher, who, with scolding brows and tightly primed shoulders, asked for the person who had scattered this theory he named brainless. Before the question could be answered, the teacher's eyes had already locked onto Theodore, frightening him with a glare that punctured his chest that was now curving inwards. Everyone in the room became quiet. They were all suddenly aware of his otherness. It wasn't the first time he had shared with the class bits of findings he thought to be interesting or comforting or fantastical and therefore impossible to keep to himself. It was recently that he had asked, in the midst of classroom silence, the question: Where am I when I am not thinking?

The teacher responded sharply, telling him that one is always thinking, and to this, Theodore paused, scratched his elbow, and responded with: But when I don't know I am thinking? As the teacher held the chin and with a cloth wiped paint from the cheeks of a child in the back of the room, he chastised Theodore's question by mockingly referring to others he had come up with in the past: if anyone had ever extracted fire from the sun, if glasses could be invented that would allow one to see time, if it was possible to photograph a scent.

It was under the shelter of the canopy by the waving willow and the maple trees where he and his friends could fantasise about reality in their own dreamful ways, free to catapult their thoughts out towards each other without the unstoppable resistance of those whose ideas they secretly wished they could battle. Under the canopy they'd speculate about points in the sky, figures on the horizon, they'd create stories for the trees, the leaves, the ladybirds, forge a purpose for the wind and twigs and tiny hills, and invent games to feed the joy of each moment where they could embody anyone they felt to be. And when beneath it alone, Theodore would ponder and wake into dreams that bent time, like when he was taken by a swift impulse to his palms and their intercrossing lines, cutting through and around one another like passages of birds drawn in the sky. They were just like the lines on the leaf he pinched between his fingers, its paper-like body spinning in circles, left, right, left, right. And he wondered what exactly lines became as they spun in the air, where they were as they hurtled in space, how multiplied their existence became as they moved, if they were no longer real for a transitory moment. Here, it didn't matter anymore that he had been made to often fear his own proclivities, for it was here where he could allow them to live boldly, at times outlandishly.

But soon, he was to meet up close the force that would hold him down, he was to discover that even the canopy would not shroud him from every sharp thing that came to puncture his perceptions, that some things would eventually follow him everywhere, to keep him behind his own current. When the day would rise, it would dawn on him that, upon waking, to be complete would not be permitted, and it would come like the arrival of an excavator sent to demolish what he had so delicately assembled through his own assessment of living. Through the instructions and the remarks of those who were grown, each day seemed to deliver a thud of disenchantment: the more time passed, the less of life there was available to him. Things he embraced began to slip away from him— whistles of melody wrenched by hard winds, far, further. Colours that had always invited him became shrouded from his gaze, light and shine were slowly replaced for the dimmed and the dark; if he was to reach for a violet, a pastel, or a muted blue, it would be replaced for a grey, a coral, a brown. Even the flowers outside that had always shone on him could elicit a smile from him no more, they were no longer for his eyes, and if he was to admire their charm he would only be reminded of that. He could no longer turn his hands into a butterfly and let his fingers flutter without a biting shame that sent them curling into small fists, and when racing along groves he could no longer spin and twirl freely in the air like the helicopter seeds he had always imitated. He had learned to stand firm, to kick balls, to run fiercely—he loved running, running had always exalted his spirit—but he felt that he could no longer run with the ribbon he had wrapped around a branch some years ago so he could watch those ethereal shapes beside his leaps that once surged wildly across the meadows. To dance with arms of bending discovery was to be mocked. To let his tears fall was to be hushed and reminded of his role to play and his growing age. To attempt to give words to the sensitivity within his chest was to be scorned and censured. He was encouraged to enjoy songs with the smallest spectrum of melody possible, and films that were gritty and sombre, and when opening his mouth to speak, what came out was soon synthesised with the knowledge of what the world expected from him, the spell that subdued him and washed the heart from his words, the very thing he needed to be in order to achieve that sense of acceptance he searched for. The yearning for the belonging he had known in the days when what he cared for, aspired, loved, was his to take hold of—it was a feeling that influenced every action of his, that never quite ceased to let go.

And to love was a limited thing, he had found. He had once witnessed the love of a beekeeper, tending sensitively to the bees, supporting their home; he had heard the sound of wedding bells, followed by laughter and chants of forever; he had wandered about the love that was inside of the rain and its perpetual pour to keep alive all the trees; at times he counted tomorrow's plans, waiting earnestly to be met with the things he cherished; he had heard "I love you" perhaps more times than he had seen the setting sun—but some loves, he discovered, were to be stifled, compressed into a narrow box where they would kick and cry to break free. In the back of the classroom on a windy afternoon, as they were reading a story about the reign of an eastern dynasty, out of nowhere he felt a hand take hold of his own. It was the hand of a friend. Her palm was cold, but against his it found warmth. He liked the feeling of it, and he closed his eyes to enlarge it. His hand had not held another in this way, and he did not want it to end, this feeling that was measureless and new, that was something akin to an extension of his own unique softness and the keeping of another's. He didn't know how to comprehend it, but he also had no need to try, so he let it happen and basked in it while he could. And on another day, in art class, he sought this feeling once more through the hand of another friend. He was sitting beside him as the two of them silently drew the little fern propped inside of the glass vase on the table. Theodore sketched with his right hand, the friend with his left, leaving their free hands to settle in the dim space beneath the table, just inches apart. Instinctively, Theodore took his hand into his own, eager to feel that merging softness again. He felt his friend's hand tighten the grasp just slightly until together they had achieved a reciprocal hold that was satisfying and round. And in that place their hands remained as they continued to draw and examine the fern, locked in a safe chamber that was like the pure calm seen in a blinking star—but, with a force that struck and pulled with might and ferocity, the star had burst, forbidden to exist on. The bond that sealed their hands had been torn. Theodore trembled, aware of the severance. He became aware that he had gone somewhere he should never have gone, that he had somehow daringly moved beyond the partition cemented before him, the partition that was now morphing into something solid as a granite rock, unmovable. He had believed that a hand was a hand, but he had learned that some were not permitted to hold, despite him and his enquiring heart, despite him and his desires that were weeping in small howls, unnoticed, unheard. He could plead for an answer, an answer as to why a thing like a care so simple and so pure could be so easily felt but forbidden to act upon. So he pleaded. He went to those who were grown and perhaps would understand why, but his pleadings were treated as nothing other than childish naivety ought to be swept away with bitter words, vague shrugs, irritation and distractions. Nothing could make him truly understand. Nothing could offer him a reason for the tearing apart of what bloomed inside of him. What followed was the shrinkage of a world that was once large, that once existed before him as a place with a pallet of a thousand colours, a place of humungous capacity, now destined to become enclosed by wrinkling walls of dust and hollow flakes of sadness. Digging his fingernails into his wrists and biting his lips until the odd taste of blood would meet his tongue, he would at times distract himself with simple pains so as to try to forget it all, to elude the callous reality that his expressions were so often forced into a mute chamber. He had discovered the sharp edges of the world, and the great rumble that seethed along the atmosphere and made his heart pound, that caused him to be afraid, incapacitated.

But in the night, when he cried beside a hushed world, he would feel it wither, like all along he had been crawling through the thickets just beyond the sore line of his affection. As he'd let himself find the night sky through the window, the mystical shades of purple behind the clouds, he'd feel the fear fade, fade and fade away, until it would seem that the crux of it was gone, that left behind was only him and his mind that approached the border of dreams and possibilities swathed in what he knew to be hope. It could come alive temporarily when he was alone with the night, when the world slumbered and the moon was lit with a wishful glow. And with it came the pulsing trust that, surely, there was more, that somewhere beyond the sphere in which he lived, even if they were only fragments he would need to hunt and seize, there had to be more. And whatever that elusive sense of more was, he did not know, but it was as if he were accompanied by a throbbing light that exposed the shadows of a corner in the hallway of thought, and if he were to tread through, he would find the corner's curve, and there he could think vaster and brighter and watch life lose its limits.

It was on a cold night of snow when he unlocked the bolt to a tiny room under the staircase. Inside the stifled space with cramped walls of chestnut wood were piles and piles of books that belonged to his parents, hidden in static shadows. He had always known this room to be a place that was not meant for his eyes, and he had respected that, never questioning it much, but on this night, something about the unreachable silence of the room and the semi-somnambulant state that had him walking into the unknown led him to wander straight into it. And it held him there, all of him and his eagerness and his nightlight of amber and gold. He perused the books, first with only his eyes, then his fingers, looking through pages and pages that were dense and unfamiliar. He was unsure what he was looking for, and the books made him feel small, and the weight of them made his young wrists throb with lack of having lived. But he had to look, for looking was his only refuge, looking might give him a key to unlock something, anything. In that night and in the nights that followed, he had learned that there did indeed exist more, so much more. In discovering this more, he had found an indication of the bigness that lived outside of his own minuscule life, a bigness that he could one day perhaps be a part of, the evidence of it in his very hands. That there were so many invisible worlds within a single one was a realisation that hadn't, until these nights, settled in him in such a lasting way. No matter how much he tried, he could not comprehend the unbounded content in the pages, but he treasured the idea of what he did not know, the mere fact that there existed a horizon beyond what he was able to recognise. Each page of every book gave life to a confirmation, a promise that he could nurture a hope that remained enclosed in his frangible mind, that somewhere written among them might be a home, for all of him. Looking into the books gifted him a calmness in waiting; owning the knowledge that each day they were just beneath his steps was like unlocking a silent yearning to the world, the world that might one day conclude teaching him how to be and instead ask him who exactly he was. It was this he yearned for. To be discovered. Like a shape of light that is just there, seen refracted onto the wall, admired, being.

The following evening had come. Gaius had been sitting perched on the table throughout the day, left alone to harden in the dry air. Unable to keep himself away for too long, Theodore had been coming back often to check the progress of solidification. He was keen to return to Yvonne and present it to her, and he hoped that by morning he'd be able to. The wind was attentive to the curtain, the vermillion one that swung beside the bookcase, dreamful. He was playing the cello in the corner of the room, the corner from which the curtain seemed to be a protective vessel behind Gaius, a soft body levitating, painting in red the message the air pursued. It was a fire with no need to burn, and so its sway could reach forever. The cello sang beneath the strings. He closed his eyes, still picturing the curtain, pouring through the black of nothing—quiet, inviting, red. And like a red howl in the room that had darkened with time, the curtain kept on billowing, a pariah amongst oak and paper. The books on the bookshelf had wandered into shadows. Gaius stood like a quiet preacher in the dark. Through the cello, Theodore had lulled his mind into an area whose depth was fluctuating and stirring like the respiration of a deathly ocean. He was called to sleep, and he yawned as he rubbed his eyes and then stood and went to Gaius to once more observe the body of clay. Delicately, he touched the hardening torso, aware of time and air converging around the mass. Taking a hold of the base, he lifted it slowly from the table. He let his eyes wander along the line between the subtle wind of movement and the clay, and then carried it to the bedroom, placing it on the windowsill. He didn't quite know why but he wanted it with him in the night. It was raining now, heavily, and behind Gaius the distorted shards of water fell hard as if deserting from a chemical reaction in the skies. Theodore lay on his bed, his hands up between his head and the pillow. Cars that were passing on the street were casting headlights through the glass of the window, projecting Gaius onto the walls as a sweeping shadow of transient existence, like a dark but hallowed breath. The room seemed to embody an anticipatory air, like it was emanating the nature of a secret, almost uttered, nearly manifested, the impatient inhalation right before the profound telling of something that would cause its habitat to shake. As Theodore's eyes were closing, slowly the room was humming and moving into a conscious dream. His being was becoming light and remote, floating into an ultra-delicate space. Not even the most delicate thing, be it the air in a case of glass, the bruise of a child, or the body of a soft coral, could have compared to his delicate sense of living. Sleep swallowed him. And, in the area that time cannot touch, a hazy scene thickened. The dream he was entering was like an ornate assembly of ice, constructed with a pin. He was aware that an iota in the movement of a finger could wake him from it, so he remained completely still, until he was no longer in the room, until he was entirely elsewhere, far gone.

A brittle wind. The scent of burnt lavender. White and indigo crystals in the air. It moved, the air, it swam, meanwhile knowing nothing other than the direction of its movement, and it was darkening with the arrival of the moon's face, all around and above like a tide of liquid fumes, journeying, cascading into itself. He didn't know where he had wandered. The road was so unfamiliar, it seemed to move in twirls through tangles of scattered trees and shrubbery, red berries and a wooden gate prancing on either side. Time felt precarious, and thin, as if it were running on steam. The atmosphere contained a sting, like its electric hands had been dispersed to point its needles into the breathing night, the night that was no longer just prescience, destined to be a thing remembered. Down in the depth he could see something booming, but its distant presence was murky and cluttered with heaps of green that had ascended from the forest. He began moving towards it, lured by possibilities, no longer bound to the string of the expected. He had a strident feeling that someone was taking him, somewhere away and untold. Soon he was following the red glide of a cloak, the cloak of that someone he had foreseen; it was like blood in the soft form of light, bending with goodness, sure of its irresistibility and the halting alarm it drew, a gleaming temptress. He was aware of no destination, but he found the darkness exhilarating, despite its foreboding edge, its tendency to be cruel and unsettling, its invisibility that at times could ruin; he found that somehow it could reveal itself like light, the way light shows its endlessness every day. The shades of darkness were plentiful, they poured over him and flooded the march of his footsteps so he was unsure if they were even real. But somehow the red of the cloak found its own place in the shelter of shadows, and it contorted into so many things: a cave bat, a sunset cloud, a hurtling moth, a ribbon, drawing a dance of ecstasy, a rhythm that could find solace in the beat of existence. Together they were chasing a melody that sounded like a row of harps submerged underneath the slow torrent of a stream, and strings that punctured, the vibrations rising out of a deep sea cave so the edges of every note were sprawling out into the widest textures; and they were floating, never staying still, constantly changing. Together they were running with the music, bleeding out their weight along the pathway. Through a cave filled with stalactite that soon became two walls enveloped with more layers of forest, they ran. Then the walls merged and before them formed a door, grand and teeming with colours that were swaying rhythmically into one another. From somewhere in the air, the person in the red cloak pulled a silver key, and with it unlocked the door that creaked with a pounding echo the second it turned. The door opened. He watched the person run through a hollow passage of stone that somehow imitated the character of water. The cloak blossomed in waves of wind, rising higher with the distance. He watched them stop at the centre point between two stone pillars descending from a ceiling that appeared as emeralds of green and violet. Theodore walked through, curious and aware of a throbbing vacillation, yet unthreatened. Through a departing mist he saw the faint outlines of other beings, forming semi-circles on both sides. Their facial features were nebulous behind a lingering white cloud of smoke. It was an orchestra, he realised. And they continued to play, louder. They had created an amphitheatre of sound with their flutes and their harpsichords and strings—violent and loving and so immediate and rare. The one in the red cloak was standing on a podium, and with a baton, they forged shapes, lines of countless measures, the spaces between stars. The music flew outwards like a cry of freedom, its heavy counterpart a large root that had been disentangled, its light counterpart a plucked petal that was levitating and meeting the intimacy of air. Then, behind the orchestra emerged voices, distant as though ascending from a faraway mountain but with a potency that came like a close whisper to an ear. He could not discern words in any particular language. It was understanding without knowing, being without realising.

The music grew louder, each component becoming a thread in a coil that was seeking to reach a point, together constructing the thinnest arrow that would prick the heart right at the centre of the song's gaze. Below the stone ceiling a circular mist was forming, pulsating with the song, growing from each part of it. The beats of his heart threw out echoes when the song reached the apotheosis, and he thought perhaps his body that was antipodal and frail could not contain such resonance, that he might not suffice to encounter the heart in the orchestration that was nothing and everything combined in a morsel of time—that he might explode and shatter into atoms. Then something grew out from his hands: a bottle of some sort, of misty blue glass that touched like ice. So piercingly cold it was on his fingers. But he had to hold on—this he somehow knew was of the most vital importance. He looked all around, then to the composer whose eyes had opened to catch sight of his own, before closing once more and returning to the music. The song had achieved the summit, he surmised. He looked up, and just below the ceiling, the haze had grown, whirling like a powder of moving particles, cyclonic, with the flairs of ink bleeding in a shaken pond, blue as purity, dark and light, and all along its spirals were painted streaks of purple and metallic silver. He knew it was his turn to do something, and by instinct, he raised the bottle up towards the mist. Its movements began to curve and run in slow circles, looping, until a shape like a funnel had been formed, the tip of it moving down, further and further until it touched the very top of the bottle. He knew that he must stay still, that any movement of the bottle would ruin the act that was taking place. Slowly the mist fell into the bottle, and the song faded into husky murmurs, and the light in the room left with it. Then the bottle was full, all of it had been captured. Behind the composer and the cloak that was descending from above, a stairway had been lit with a glow of tamed gold. With the bottle firmly clenched, Theodore walked to the composer, wondering loudly with his eyes if he was to take the bottle up the stairway. He could see a face now, gracious in the sparse light, eyes wise and alluring, a mouth that lent the smile an elegant sureness. The composer bowed their head subtly and then turned to face the stairway. Theodore was certain now of his next step, so he made his way over there and walked carefully to the top. Up there was nothing but another pathway leading to clouded darkness. He walked the tiniest footstep inwards and suddenly a light that fell from above cast a spotlight in the near distance, down onto a figure who was of a great size and a strange matter of skin, who lay stuck to the ground like a fallen shadow, sleeping, who, through a squint in the eyes, was almost certainly Gaius. But he was large, much larger than Theodore himself, who quietly but vehemently shuddered with blinding shivers. His feet froze above a wobbling ground. His fingers clasped so mightily onto the bottle it surprised him that it did not shatter. He looked back downwards for guidance, but the composer and the orchestra were gone. It was only him now, him and this untamed, deistic creature he had made. A bird cawed in the sky. He looked down at the mist that had somehow condensed into a liquid, restful in the bottle like a breathing topaz. He was suddenly reminded that he could wake if he wished to, that with just the opening of his eyes he could obliterate it entirely, but despite the fear, he couldn't refrain from settling into the dream, from keeping alive the fable and arriving at the ending. He moved one, two, three steps forward, paused, then walked a little more. Aware of no movement ahead, he thought perhaps Gaius was sound asleep, but as he came closer he couldn't discern a single hint of breath. He wondered if Gaius was dead, and if his undertaking was to revive him by providing him with the elixir in the bottle, the grand concerto that was now in liquid form. A few more steps forward he walked, then some more, until Gaius lay just a little in front of him. He recognised the details of the clay body, the very imprints his fingers had formed, and those facial features he had gotten to know. With a tremble, he reached his hand to touch the face. It was solid as rock, but the surface was smooth to touch, a hard satin. Defying the fear, he pinched the chin, holding it in his fingers as if it were a piece of fruit, and with a slow force, he pulled down the jaw, opening the mouth which revealed a shadowed vacuum of absent breath. Then, over the mouth, he tilted the bottle slightly, seeing the first tiny gush of liquid fall in. He waited a few seconds until silence returned. Again, he fed the mouth of Gaius, bit by bit letting it all fall in until he had emptied the bottle. Silence again. Nothing moved, nothing formed a sound. He stood up and waited. A chilly angst caressed him all over, and trying to stifle it was like trying to silence a furious animal, so he let it happen, until he found that it was merged with a faint hope. And then a rumble, like a growl without a voice, came from the ground, from Gaius. He watched the entire clay body release a tremor that with every second grew. The ground began to quake, violently. Theodore bolted straight to the stairway and down the stairs, running to the podium and grasping it with all of his might. The shaking intensified, spreading across the entire area, and he closed his eyes and with his struggling body hugged the podium and waited. Seconds—minutes. When calm returned and the tremors had subsided, he opened his eyes. All was silent now other than a far-flung bird, it's call like the chime of a pleading bell. He turned around and looked to the stairway. His gaze moved up and up the steps, and at the very top he saw the shape of Gaius's tall figure looking down on him, a stance of thunder. He was alive, wildly. Theodore froze all over. He had often known life to fluctuate somewhere between beauty and devastation, but in this moment the two counterparts had converged, for he was both mesmerised and terrified, ecstatic and nauseated, enlivened and set ablaze.

It was through this amalgamation that he opened his eyes. He needed some moments to breathe before he could move any part of him. He was seeing the room now as if he had just turned his eyes away from the lens of a telescope, hypnotised by a planet's orbit. Mulling over the details of the dream in this fragile state of mind was like holding onto the limbs of memory as it is ferociously lured into a forgotten void. He recalled every moment of it, giving the pictures weight and colour so he would not forget, so all of it would remain intact. A stirring heat was above him, thick and humid and in every spot of air that he breathed. The morning light was beginning to make itself seen. He got up, slowly, hoisting himself up and towards the window. He turned the handle and pushed it wide open, feeling the breeze on his face. Then he pulled back his arm, but in doing this—it had happened so abruptly he hadn't even time to realise—he had struck the side of Gaius with his elbow. It crashed to the ground, breaking into pieces that, because of the dark, Theodore could not see. But he heard all of it, every break and crack, the shattering and the rolling of hard clay beside his feet, the ending of the cherished sculpture who had lived for nothing more than two nights.

PART III

Wandering through the rooms of an ancient history museum, Theodore had once imagined the tumbling of bones of prehistoric creatures: the ribs, the backbones, the tails, breaking away to the floor, how they would pile like a mound of sad crumbled architecture. This fall of Gaius was perhaps the closest thing he had witnessed to that gut-wrenching sensation he had felt in his knees and his stomach. It was the sound of the fall that punctured him so viscerally, the hitting and the breaking, and the mental image of each piece scattering, some beneath a wardrobe, others under the bed, the unlucky ones combusting into particles and getting lost in the wefts of the nearby rug. Immediate light of dawn poured in as he drew open the curtains. Looking down, he saw perhaps seven or eight pieces of clay, broken around the armature. To his fortune there were no shattered chips, no fragmented limbs in hundreds of pieces; there was only a severed head, a torso torn in three, a sheared arm, a broken leg at the knee, a foot ripped asunder. And despite the odd and perverse image below him, by virtue of the slightest hint of softness on the wooden floor, the damage was much less severe than he had imagined. Taking each broken piece into his hands, he examined them closely, wondering with a focussed sight. He thought perhaps if he were somehow able to soften the clay once more he could remould it from the unworked clump it used to be, but then he decided, abruptly, that to erase this unique form would be an abysmal thing to do; it would be wiser to dispose of it as a fractured body of parts that certainly still contained the essence of the character. But to get rid of it just like that, without any attempt to repair, would be the deed of a half-hearted person, he thought. His adoration for the sculpture was stronger than the urge to give up, so he would try, he would figure out a way to fix this. Through morning light, he looked out to the trees, waving pinecones and red beads, rustling dearly through gusts on which robins with shimmering necks hovered. He thought about Yvonne, and that perhaps she could help him, that with some luck she'd own a little tub of glue designated for an accident such as this, a glue that would doubtlessly bring the pieces together, make Gaius whole once more. So he distracted himself to let the morning rise, and then he got ready and left, without any more thought, each piece of clay placed in a shoebox he stuffed and padded with a woven cloth.

On foot, her place was only some fifteen minutes away, but to Theodore it seemed to be much less, for his walk was patched with a skip that made him bounce with avidity. The gloom that had lurched onto him at the falling of Gaius had departed. It dawned on him that ever since the night before yesterday he had somehow deviated onto a path of unfolding surprise, that with every passing instant there seemed to grow, out of nothing, avenues whose insides were draped in multicolour. Nature and its secrets had rarely appeared so alluring, had rarely consisted of so many faces, and he couldn't recall a time when he had been so affected by its many patterns and contortions. He could feel a stark perceptivity, and that each breath passing through him skimmed the reflection of all that he could possibly imagine. But he was restful, while ready at any moment to divulge a great expression, like a nightingale who waits for the pointed whisper of dusk to call for its emphatic cry. So he took his unweighted self there, and when he arrived he waited at the door after ringing the bell, once, twice. No ring was answered. And then he heard, just perceptibly, the echoes of piano from above. He knew it was coming from Yvonne's flat, for he remembered how she would often listen to piano in the calm hours of day. Before thinking to ring her, he had the idea of throwing tiny twigs up to her window to try to catch her attention, something they used to do when visiting each other those years ago. At the base of a tree he found a handful and threw them up to the window, one by one, attempting a gentle tap on the glass each time. Moments passed and the window did not open. He laughed and whistled a sustained howl like that of a crying kettle, foolishly thinking perhaps it would pierce through the wafting piano. And just after throwing up another twig and watching it pirouette in the air before pouncing with a light tap on the glass, the window opened and out popped Yvonne's astonished face.

— Come up here, Goose!

He remembered now that the two of them would amusingly address one another as Goose, although he couldn't recall where the name had come from. Hearing it now was like opening a happy pocket of the past, one that had been seamed by stitches through time.

— I should have called, he said when he got to the door.

He observed that the music was in fact coming from above, for inside Yvonne's home was only the sound of a breeze sensitively rustling the fig tree by the window, just one among the many plants and floras now held in artisanal position. Yvonne welcomed him, then walked into the open kitchen, returning to cartons of berries that she washed and tossed into a treen bowl, her demeanour bright and transparent.

— Share with me your great dilemma, she called to him, a shine in her voice.

On the living room table, Theodore placed down the broken sculpture, and then each piece carefully around the armature, laying them down to rest in a semi-circle.

— Here. My rare opus.

In walked Yvonne, wiping berry stains from her hands. A gasp escaped her and her eyes flashed a profusion of delight, and she went over to the table and, with the embrace of her fingers, gave the broken thing her sweetest admiration. There was something Theodore noticed about the way she touched the pieces: as if they were breathing elements with subtle observations of their own. And there was a spout of care in the focus she gave that made him wish to treasure the moment. It was the often undetected wanting to sustain a passing moment in time that makes one feel they are truly in the right place, like reaching to stroke the plumage of the moment's wings that glide along by, ephemerally. A bitter thing that is nonetheless so sweet.

— You made this?

The voice behind her question was hushed and honeyed.

— The other night, after you fell asleep, something came over me and I couldn't resist getting my hands in the clay. Soon after I started putting it together I just couldn't stop. And this was the result.

Yvonne shook her head, amused and perplexed, then leant closer as she inspected the broken parts with finer precision.

— What happened?

— Earlier this morning, I had just woken from a dream, and, in a daze, I knocked him off the windowsill. I thought I'd bring him here, that maybe you'd have an idea about how to fix him.

— We'd have to get a hold of some ceramic glue. I've seen a place down the street where we can likely get some.

As she turned towards the window to look out, she paused.

— Wait. I may have a better idea. Yesterday, as I was arriving home, I saw through the windows of the floor above me, on top of piles of books, these ceramic ornaments that were lined with golden streaks. They were so beautiful that I halted for a minute so I could take a look at them from afar. Have you heard of kintsugi?

— No, I don't think I have, said Theodore.

— It's a Japanese art of filling the cracks of broken pottery, usually with some sort of golden gluey substance, a lacquer or something.

She paused, hummed and murmured something to herself, then turned to him.

— How adventurous are you feeling? She seems like a kind old lady, the one who lives upstairs. I'm thinking you could go up there and ask her. I'm sure she would be able to help. Just imagine how this would take form if the spaces were filled with gold.

— You think she wouldn't mind?

— I doubt it. The other day I caught a glimpse of her sweeping the hallway. She was in her own world, smiling with this slow wonderment that she didn't even take notice of anyone walking by.

Theodore looked to Gaius, the body like disfigured rocks fallen from a precipice. He imagined the sight of golden lacquer between the spaces, and the thought of it lit him inside with a scintillating urge, to go and try.

— I'll ask her.

As he ascended the stairs in the hallway, Yvonne standing by the door to listen out from below, he was thrilled by the growing sounds of piano, and at the same time he took notice of an unexpected scent, a sweet aroma that touched with an edge of something unknown, like a strange fruit containing the ripest syrup, infused with the scent of pungent earth. Towards the very top, each stair whimpered a creak that deepened with weight. And at the door, he knocked softly but firmly, Gaius tucked in the shoebox in his arms. After a few breaths he heard what sounded like approaching footsteps, and then silence, a drawn-out silence in which he became sure that his warped silhouette was being inspected through an eye in the peephole. And just as the silence reached a point that prompted him to leave, with a small succession of sliding metal locks, slowly, the door opened, and out of a hollow darkness that was lit in small glitters by rays of a stained glass lamp in the blurred background, an old, small in height, stern but soft face looked up to him. The face cast a fleeting but indelible first impression: the dark and slanted eyes, white and dishevelled hair, magenta-painted lips constellated by moles and wrinkles, a fluffed chin creased with unusual speculation.

— Yes?

The word was extended and began deep and grand but bent into a raised pitch that ended with a whispered squeak. Theodore stuttered before clearing his throat and speaking.

— Hi... I hope I'm not intruding. I'm Theodore. I'm a friend of Yvonne, who lives downstairs. We noticed you have some mended pottery by your window, and you see, we have a small problem here, he said as he opened the box and tilted it towards her unwavering glare. I came up to ask if you'd have an idea about how we can fix this. Any advice would really help.

Through squinted eyes, she looked into the box. She was focussed, so focussed it was almost as if with her eyes she had dispelled his presence completely. Then, through her throat, she made a coarse grumble that implied a vague contemplation, looked up to him, then turned around and headed back into her home, the door closing behind her. Moments passed. Theodore remained still, losing certainty with every second that she would return. Until she did, abruptly, and with a magnifying glass she looked into the box, picking up and examining some of the pieces, a stern twitch in her beady eye that did not once blink. She was mumbling, unintelligibly, and then she reclined and nodded, an indistinct grin in her demeanour.

— I can fix it.

Theodore sighed, thankfully.

— Really, you can? he said, before reaching into his pocket. Here, let me pay you something.

— No, money is not necessary, she said, shooing away his proposition with her hands as she turned, before pausing to think. But maybe a small favour in return?

— Of course, anything.

— Excellent, she said, amusingly. You can come in now.

With a playful huff, she tugged on his sleeve a few times, gesturing for him to enter. So he did, a small hesitancy in his step, a feathered throb of anticipation in his chest. And immediately as the door was shut behind him, he found that he was now enclosed in a world unlike any other he had known, for the entrance hall before him was a concoction made from perhaps the wildest imagination he had met, detailed with uncountable facets. The circular pieces that constituted the floor were logs of sienna wood, flattened and converging and specked with the shuffled marks on the trees of a fruitful orchard. On the walls were paintings whose colours appeared to almost hover above the panels, and hanging textiles connected to strings of twine, gliding below the ceiling from which small ornamental artefacts hung. Lampshades of bronze and paisley and gems, painted and tasselled, appeared to float above their heads. In a corner of the ceiling, he saw flakes of crumpled newspaper thrown over and around one another, yellowed and faded by time. And then a cat, noticeably the same cat that had appeared in Yvonne's place, strutted along the doorway, its shadow engraving the stained glass, its tail like a stalk in the wind. It jumped onto an upright piano and lay there to rest beside a porcelain vase that was blotted with orbs of blue and forest green.

The old woman walked with a large stick in her hand that she held like a sceptre. Into the living room Theodore followed. He was in a misty sort of daze, his mind in a puff of cloud that made the moment feel painted in dripping technicolour—and he adored it. Along the walls, hundreds upon hundreds of books were piled and stacked, a tamed chaos of paper upon paper. And by the windows and on the shelves were ceramics—vases, pots, jugs, sculptures of distinct proportions, many of them broken and mended with gold seamed along the cracks. From a hexagonal table of chipped and battered wood, Theodore watched her brush away scraps and crumples of ink-filled paper onto the floor with a glide of the arm.

— Put the poor thing on here, she said in a crucial whisper.

Theodore halted.

— What about all your papers?

— Never mind them. That story has been running around in circles. It will likely never see the light of day.

— You write? he asked as he placed the pieces of Gaius onto the table.

— Occasionally I write stories, among other things.

Theodore pointed to the gold-mended jar sitting in the hearth before them.

— Kintsugi, right?

— Yes, you see, I break them and I repair them. It starts like this.

He hadn't any time to see from where she had picked up a hammer before he watched her suddenly hurl it towards a large vase that stood upon a stool beside them. The cacophony of the impact sent him jumping and his arms flailing as he watched the broken pieces of clay fall to the floor in fractured shapes, like those of countries on a map. Placing the hammer down, she laughed triumphantly and sighed and then spoke:

— That was for the sake of demonstration. I usually wait for the clamour of traffic outside the window to do that.

— So you break them yourself? he asked, his face etched with disbelief.

— I break them and then I repair them, she replied, markedly pleased.

She knelt and touched the pieces with her hands, the tips of her fingers finely stroking the jagged edges of the breaks.

— It is the process of thoughtless destruction into delicate attention. The breaking is the concentrating of ferocity, letting the desire for annihilation pass through the hammer onto the object. And to repair is to mend, to nurture with a careful hand, and to bring the object back to life, as an even more captivating, complex form. A vase like this one will never break in the same way. I could destroy thousands of them and I will always find new intricacies, and that is what I accentuate, that is what I seek to give the gold to.

She stood up and dusted herself off.

— It will take some time to repair your sculpture. I will need to work on this a little bit each day in order to let the pieces dry, untouched. Give me two weeks.

Theodore, naturally lost in observation, watched her trace the outline of the pieces with her finger in the air. He snapped out of it as she looked to him.

— And what about the favour? he asked.

— Ah, yes, the favour!

She walked across the room and out from one of many draws took out a package wrapped in beige paper and sealed with a bowed string.

— I would like you to get this delivered for me. It's a package for a friend of mine and I'd like to get it to them as soon as possible. The postal service is just around the corner, a small walk from here.

She handed him the package.

— I know this place, he said, looking at the written address on the front. It's only an hour away on the train. If you'd like me to get it there today, I could even go and deliver it myself.

— If you enjoy throwing yourself into a journey like that, even better.

And then the two of them looked towards those broken pieces of clay in the shoebox, their thoughts perhaps aligned in wordless admiration.

— I named the sculpture Gaius, said Theodore, smiling easily.

— Gaius! she called, smacking her palms and her wrists together in a distinct rhythm as she walked back to the hallway.

He followed her through, until, at the doorway, she stopped, and from a hook in the wall took a necklace of stone pendants in bountiful shapes and shimmers, and placed them around his neck, humming a slight, indistinct song as she did so.

— Now, go. Come and knock on my door in two weeks and I will have fixed your sculpture.

He headed out, and, at the door, called goodbye to her as she stood in the hallway, her hands surging along the piano beneath the sleeping cat, her fingers tracing a wave before returning to the keys.

— But, oh—I didn't ask for your name?

— Himari! she called.

— Himari, he whispered after closing the door.

He went straight down to Yvonne, who burst into gasps and laughter of surprise as he told her about the interaction. And then, so as not to waste a minute, he left.

The outside was stirring a breeze that lulled the trees, and so along with the wind's whistle, a great rustling was heard, and along with that the pigeons and starlings and sparrows hurled their silent bodies in lines that dashed and curved, before landing on chimneys to see from above the teeming splinters of town below. Theodore felt the eager call of the day gushing through him with the morning gale, hurtling with waves of shawms and cymbals, like those that climb the walls of a colosseum. And in this state of sensitivity, he was called to the current of the very instant that was reverberating with potentiality, conveying the way the clouds ceaselessly reveal the tone of the sky. And he became aware of that same particular jounce in his step; he moved through the day as if a quartet played a song to which his feet bobbed along. On the street he bubbled with a reverberation that was like the ripples of stone-skipped water, and with this brightened mood he made his way to the train station and boarded the train.

Light of the sun came filtering through leaves, skittering along sideways with the freckles of rosebush and distant buttercups on hills with arches that were swallowed by speed, an alchemical sight. In a poignant silence, small things that came into vision through the window carried with them pieces of his memory. A windmill, as it made circles that skimmed the furrows of wheat, reminded him of a particular memory by a cottage beside a windmill just like it, where, along the passing lakes, he had picked rocks: agate, granite, unakite. In the cottage, within the light of a candelabrum, he keenly inspected the patterns and the colours of the little rock bodies. It was the first time he had sat to appreciate something as banal as a rock, and in doing so not only had he inflated the margin of their beauty, but he had brightened a new penchant of his. As the train swept by fields, a herd of deer in a passing enclosure, with their white speckles and antlers of distinct curves, took him back to a far-off but unclouded memory: a time he had wandered with his small feet to see up close the fawns in the lofty grass. He remembered his father's call from the car as he realised he had gone too far, and the mother deer appearing from behind a tree, aggression in the face and hooves as they struck the ground impetuously. He had frozen, struck by a thunder-quick dread he had not formerly known. A shadowy faintness had come upon him as he watched the mother deer stomp with ferocity her long legs to the ground again and again as a lurking wind tousled the leaves and the sun disappeared behind a cloud, cloaking the entire field in a moody grey spell. He had turned around, straight into his father's arms, whose desperate calls, vacant with horror, had not penetrated the hypnotism he was under; it was a deep and frightful trance in which he had come to realise that there existed much more beyond what his judgement assumed, that a deer like the one before him, despite its pretty exterior, was in fact a weighted existence comprised of many more sensitivities and characteristics than meets the eye, among them angst and violent passions. As the train bent along the tracks and the rocking side to side escalated, he saw not too far away what looked like a water well with a wooden roof above a round structure of stone. It was just like the well he had noticed as a young adolescent in the far distance on a family trip. He had gone up to inspect it, with some of his older cousins by his side, who, when he went to reach for the bucket, pulled him back in a fearful outburst. He had wished to discover the groundwater, to see what he might bring up to the surface, but their fear of the dark unknown below had crept into him and muddied his instinct. Thinking back, he remembered how on that very same excursion he had wished to explore a hedge maze that came into sight, and he had asked an older relative if they'd like to join him. Refusing to let him go in, they had told him that they would never step foot in there, and upon insisting, they immediately took hold of his arm and whisked the idea away with an axiom: that oftentimes life is similar to thrashing one's way through a maze, with nettles and thorns in every corner waiting to spear you down and stifle you so it feels almost impossible to escape its edges. Although, at the time, these words had left a mark on him and his growing sensibility, he found humour in recapturing all of it now.

As he admired the passing bluebells he thought of Himari, how blunt and charismatic she was. Rarely did he meet anyone so magnetising, whose home stood as a mirrored image of their own distinctiveness. And this small expedition of his had seemingly come out of nothing; the day had unfurled into something so out of the ordinary that it could almost have grown from the stem of a daydream—and it was still morning. And then there was Yvonne; he hadn't yet reflected much on their meeting, and now, as the train carried his body in frills of motion, he could do nothing but smile as he thought of her. The distant past had never seemed so within his mind's reach. He remembered how, after the few years they had spent in each other's company, life slowly started to steer them in opposite directions. He had felt the urge to travel Europe, she Asia; he had been called to chase a career, she a change of lifestyle; he had merged parts of his life with other friends, she had gotten involved with someone romantically and so gave much of her time to them. Soon, when they were to meet again, something was starkly different: it was as if one of them, or perhaps both of them, were not speaking what was meant to be spoken. Perhaps a sadness was not expressed, a refusal to acknowledge how much they had relied on one another; perhaps there was a lack of vulnerability in trying to prove a point, avoidances and equivocations; perhaps there was a projection of confusion, a mood of reservation between them, turmoil that had not been tended to. Or it could have been all of those things. What had followed was a slow distancing, a fading away, and eventually, out. But all of it now, these years later, he could see, was a clear indication that the two of them needed to understand their own selves through a finer lens, to learn to communicate resolutely, in a way that did not cloud the observable, that all that was needed was time apart to let one another become the people they were now. He could feel churning from inside the knowing that what they had, the very thing that tied their minds together, still existed, and that with time they would get back to that pure place of relation, that they would eventually talk about it all, everything that had happened, with clear hindsight of reflection, and what would come out of it would be whole and pure, and rare. And rare was indeed the word, for her presence to him had always been one that pushed him beyond convention, the patterns of normality, to a region of mind where insight and eccentricity and vibrant ideas are formed, right where he knew he belonged—and still it was now.

He was staring, peering out at the wideness through the window as if every detail were a message, a dot in the conglomeration of a dream—a dream, like many, whose textures would be swiftly forgotten with waking eyes. Quite unlike the dream that had visited him the night before; somehow the memory of it came back to him as if it lay within the memory of just a few seconds ago, and now it had settled so he knew he would remember it forever if he chose to. It was tightly sealed, ineffaceable. The only part he could not recall was the song of the orchestra; the melody had been washed away in the tide of a mind realising its own self again as it wakes to find light. But he could scarcely recall the feeling of it, the pale tremor it had created in the root of him, the fact that it had held him, all of him and his brittle beating heart. And the image of Gaius in that large and unstoppable form, his courageous eyes beckoning from above—the mere recollection of it now sent his hair raising and his nerves twitching. In the night he moulded the clay, to attempt to understand why he did it was like trying to understand time by hearing only the ticking of the clock. Now, he wondered, through a feeling that came over him in a soft suddenness: what is Gaius? If not just a sculpture like many others, from a bucket of clay that would perpetually carry an eternity of more, if not a solid shape that could take the role of filling the space on a shelf, where it would occasionally be forgotten behind the wind-blown curtain, a tiny part in a larger picture, to which eyes would stare, if not for a single second, then maybe two or three, with the occasional futile touch of a finger. If it wasn't any of that, and clearly to him it couldn't be, then what was it? His desire to treat the sculpture as a thing that breathed the sound of life, as if it were carved for something with a purpose beyond its structure, and the glint and the pulse he had felt at the creation of it, the pulse that was more than a heartbeat, now made him aware of the great mystery of it, the mystery of why such a small thing could elicit so much. But sooner than he could find the next thought, the abstraction vanished as distance and speed distracted him.

He stepped off the train beside hills of abundant green. The sun was a diadem in the sky, holding the poise of a god. He walked down a road with a character unknown. He saw distant hedges like stagnant green smoke, a parked van with olive trees and lemonade, a hare that skittered through a busy plot of land. The stone pathway on which he walked drew bends along the expanse like a curl in the cry of woodwind. As he moved he took a long look at the package, the small rectangular structure, shaking it a little to find an indication of what it could be. But he delighted in the weight and the shape of it, in the question of its undefined being that perhaps was unfolding, slowly.

A short walk led him to the location. A house of stone, surrounded by apricot trees and a fence of bamboo firmly secured along the edges. A candle's jouncing flicker burned through the window, a tiny illumination that shone with novelty and at the same time like a fleck of a strangely familiar call. Someone in flowing linen and ruffled hair was sat on the bench of an arbour by the wall of the house, leaning into a bunch of papers, and as Theodore drew nearer, the person looked up to him, revealing a sweet face of surprise, composed and curious. His brows were thickly waved, and below them, two alabaster eyes peered with generous, questioning anticipation. From his ears dangled two stones of amber, and from his neck, a cloth like a wilted flower hung to life. He was seemingly younger than Himari, but much older than Theodore, who cleared his throat to speak.

— Sorry to interrupt your reading, but I— I've come with a delivery, from Himari.

He gave him the package, watching his expression grow bigger and brighten as he held it with affection, his forefinger skimming the string with a feathery pressure. Then he looked up.

— And who are you?

His voice was like melodic air.

— I'm Theodore. I live near Himari. I told her I'd bring this to you.

Then, leaning back into the bench, he nodded, his eyes diverting for a second as a welt of wind shook the leaves, perhaps up to the sky, or to the plump apricots, nearing their time for plucking.

— I'm Cadeo, he said quietly, intentionally. Thank you for bringing this to me.

Imbued with an automatic impulse to turn around and say goodbye and think nothing more of the interaction, Theodore turned himself away just slightly, but, quite like a spark of flint, something arrived on him with clarity: he became distracted by a certain fascination, a fascination set alight through a synchronisation of forces, one of them being the ever-moving trailing plants of red and copper, enveloping the sight of nearness, another being Cadeo's demeanour that was like an open stream made up of tiny smiling rivulets. And so he spoke:

— I hope you don't mind my prying, but I can't help but wonder, what's inside the package?

And for an instant he thought perhaps his wondering had probed him a little too far, for the question wasn't responded to right away. Cadeo looked up to him, his eyes squinting behind eyelashes as sunlight beckoned from behind.

— In here, he said, tapping on the box, is a song.

He began opening it, first by unravelling the string, then by slowly tearing away the paper. He removed the lid from a small wooden box that was like a hand-sized treasure trove, and inside, encased in a transparent cover, was a cassette tape.

— Ah, music! said Theodore. Is it a song of hers?

Cadeo gestured for Theodore to sit beside him, perhaps observing the wideness of his interest, and so he did. He too leant back into the arbour, feeling his body resting beneath the leaves and branches, his breath exiting him like silken blossoms running with the air. Cadeo spoke:

— I paint. I've been a painter for most of my life. It must have been thirteen or fourteen years ago now when this happened. I had lost my paintings in a fire, years and years of my work, all gone, and I was going through a season of grief. For so long I had treasured what I painted, I had kept each painting safely locked away so the world could never harm them. After losing them, for a long time I no longer had it in me to paint—I was emptied, too distracted by hurt. I starved myself of opportunity, I wept in parks and empty meadows and train stations, searching for what used to kindle the urge in me, yearning for that sense of creation. I wanted to find myself again, to let in light after loss. This slow period eventually passed, and I, gradually, began to paint again. A friend of mine had opened up a café down by the coast, and we had put one of my paintings there on display. It was large, and we had it hung up on a wall beside hanging baskets of flowers that overlooked one of those old steinway-pianos.

He stopped talking and took a moment to look at Theodore with a puzzle in the pinch of his stare. Perhaps, Theodore thought, he was attempting to ascertain his interest in finding more. So he raised his brows and lifted his eyes, parading his desire to listen. Cadeo stared off into the distance for a few seconds, then began again:

— One day I came by to visit the café, and my friend eagerly handed me a cassette tape. He had been waiting for me to come by so he could give it to me. He told me that an old woman had walked in one afternoon, drank some tea, then sat by the piano. For a long time she sat there, and the entire time her eyes were set on my painting above. She was playing the piano, just sitting there, moving her ringed fingers along the keys without once taking her eyes off the painting. The sound of her music moved my friend to tears. He asked her if he could document it, and she agreed, and so he put a tape recorder on a nearby table and had it recorded. When she finished playing he asked her for the name of the song. What she responded with astonished me. It was the painting, she told him. The song she played was what, in that moment, the painting had given her. Of course, I was surprised and delighted to hear this, so I took the tape home and listened to it, here in this exact spot, among the buds of early spring. As soon as I pressed play and heard the opening notes, I was met with awe, taken to a dream that I did not leave until the click that marked the end. I listened to it again and again, like a gift I had always wished to hold. It contained this field of unearthly notes in perpetual motion, an atmosphere in which I could somehow hear a sense of home. I held onto it, and whenever I'd wish to be reminded of it, I'd listen. Somehow, whenever I'd listen to it, a new face would appear among the keys, a new feeling would kindle, I'd discover new thoughts of abstraction from somewhere in the music. I had thought that I'd known it, but each time it played I found that I didn't quite know it in its entirety. Each note, each chord, the spaces between them, the falling and rising, the contrasting tones, the impulse of every phrase, every bend, every lilt—each aspect of it was a twig in a vast tree. Sure, I could assign it certain lineaments and features, but I came to realise that that would be limitary when attempting to listen to what it was truly speaking of. It was a realisation I had one morning, a couple of years later. I hadn't heard the song in a long time, and something about the freshness of that day made me think of it. I listened again. This time it appeared differently, in an entirely new way. I felt a keen sense that it was giving me something, something with which to use, something with which to paint. So I did, immediately I set up a wooden panel and threw paint onto it, and in such a way that I hadn't yet experienced. The strokes of the paintbrush did not matter to me, for it was only that which was true to the song that was showing up. That was all that mattered. Until then I had always painted what I saw before me. I had painted scenery through the contents of my mind—a sunset over town, a river of anchored boats, a glade in sunlight—but now I was doing something completely different, I was painting the meeting point between what I was hearing and all the ways it made me feel. Just like she had composed my painting, I was now painting her composition. I was creating the very form of colour the music was giving to me through that particular moment. When it fell into completion, I wanted nothing more than to give it to her. But I knew nothing about her. So I left it sitting above the mantlepiece. It wasn't until a couple more years later, after she had fortuitously visited the café again and my friend had recognised her and managed to get her information, that I wrote to her. I told her that I wanted to give her the painting, that I had painted it to the song she had played those years ago. She wrote back to me. She told me she remembered playing it. She told me how my painting had reminded her of those by someone she loved who had passed away, how seeing it had caused a familiar movement inside of her. Soon I had the new painting sent to her. I expected nothing back, and that was all, for a while. Then, months passed, and I received a small package, like this one. It was another cassette tape, with a little note. On it, she wrote telling me that she had, once again, composed a song to the painting I had given to her. I remember listening to it with tears in my eyes, finding something beautiful and undiscovered inside of it. I would listen to it here and there, and when I felt that familiar impulse arrive, I painted it, just like I had painted the other one, the very way I heard it. Again, I sent the painting to her. And once again, some months passed, and then I received a new tape from her. I was overjoyed that she too wished to keep on going back and forth with this strange form of communication. So back to her I painted, and back to me she composed. My paintings were no longer a thing to merely be made, they were movement, sensorial movement. Together we had created an ever-evolving conversation that happened for years and years, and is still somehow happening now.

Cadeo cleared his throat. His story had sung like a harp and then crashed and deepened into a fissure of water. Theodore was at a halt of silence. That he could often be so touched by the stories of others was a trait of his so finely engraved within, but no story had touched him quite like this one in the longest time; it was the contact of words that contained a past so chasmic that one is swallowed by the mere sound, the pricking of a mammoth's tusk.

— Wow, he faintly murmured.

There was not much he could say, and perhaps sensing his mute astonishment, Cadeo stood up, holding the tape up in the diamond light, his face in the shade of purple blossoms.

— Would you like to listen to this one, together?

Theodore sat hushed, for words now evaded him. And in finding comfort in the colours of the background, and Cadeo, and his own soft way of seeing, he nodded and rose to his feet.

— I'd like that a lot.

Cadeo took him inside amongst a variety of belongings that appeared to emit a feeling of home. A vigorous warmth lay beside everything. Then he lit a candle, the sound of the matchstick a hiss that preceded an ease he recognised like the touch of a familiar hand. The flicker was large and in tentative waves, a solitary display of light that skirted along the earthenware and the painted ochre along the walls. They sat by a table next to the window, where Cadeo set some tea in a crafted teapot and, in the centre, placed the tape recorder. Alongside the distant thrumming of a nearby train, the tape recorder hissed, and out came a shuffling and a creaking and a ruffling of fabrics, and then a seamless ring of a piano key, and a high octave, before the pouring in of deep, speculative chords. Then, in tandem with a stirring wind in the pit of Theodore's chest that was both serene and incomprehensible, a succession of higher melodies came through like air, followed by weighty harmonies between the low and the high, sustained by the imperceptible throb of the pedal. On and on it went to paint the landscape of a song, unfolding like lucent echoes that leapt and howled in response to one another. He looked at Cadeo, whose eyes were closed, his pupils attuned to the sound, and his mind, whilst it circumnavigated the song, bending between the fringes of the notes, would likely remain there until the end, Theodore surmised, the end that would not be soon, nor late, for time was now hooked and each minute destined to curve. This was a moment set apart from any other, the closest thing in his memory being a time he looked out to the view of a night-gowned ocean and watched, with unrelenting mesmerism, a tiny, flaring dot in the offing slowly grow into the diamond-chiselled light of a lantern attached to the tip of a canoe that soon arrived on the shore —a moment in which time had become flooded with wonder and speculation so it could not carry out its usual measure, it could no longer glide along ground, but hover. So comforting it was that in the song he could go anywhere, for nothing held him down, and soon his gaze locked onto the steam that encircled the rim of the mug in front of him. As if reaching for nothing, it flared and vanished again and again, reckless and in the motions of a gale that could be seen. Through an inward and weightless tremor, he glided, the steam gliding with him, to a memory captured by the eyes of his child-self, the past blurting out swiftly, fogging the line of the present. In the memory, smoke, reminiscent of the circling steam, rose above a hand, a hand that he noticed resembled a swan, the two pinching fingers as the neck, the rest of it as the body and wings in a rested pose on a plane of a wandering lake. And perhaps he too could embody this swan, he remembered thinking as he watched its story unfurl, finding vast intricacies inside of it. He saw the hand paint endless shapes of conversation as it conducted the smoke, as if it were performing as a dandelion in a windstorm, the two fingers in a minuet, and the smoke like whirlpools of clouds that had evaporated time, smoke in ripples of humour, smoke like that of dreams, smoke curling towards her lover's fingertips, her lover's skirt, her lover's eyes, eyelashes. And eyelashes gently collided in fleeting swoops over pupils with an endless glimmer, a glimmer he wished his eyes would contain as they saw the world and caught glimpses of what lived inside of him in each day. Approaching with a slow immediacy, he noticed a vague, but not unfelt, sensation that was bitter and murky and unpleasant, something he had associated with the disillusionment of his younger years. Coldness circulated like dead fingers fluttering a lifeless hymn. Somewhere in the rising steam, he saw an inlet of air, like a ravine, the sides turning and opening, forming a route that would lead somewhere. And upon looking deeper, he could have sworn it was leading him to a place beneath it, that inside was a route to a voice whose words were firm and opaque; it was as if it were calling him, luring him so it could whisper to him a message, telling him: here, here is the sense of what it means to live through a heart with the tinting of haze, with the opacity of nothing but dormant, storm-ridden clouds; tread through and you will find the insipid memories of suppressed tears above your cheeks— so plump with youth they are, not once suspecting the twisted reality that will soon strike them—and the subtle swell of the throat below the gnashing of newly blooming teeth, your teeth, those pearly studs of finely shaped bone that chewed through the stammers of anguish. In it, he had arrived at the story he had once abandoned, the story of his own strain and despair, and it could not have been any clearer than it was here, for he let it pour, respire, insistently—upon him. Now he was going in, he was entering the ravine, and more memories were bursting forth like triggers of rolling thunder, memories that could not be measured. A sunken, bitter sadness came to touch him, a feeling he recognised as what was good and pure turning away from him before his very eyes, the perpetual finding out that the world was not quite how he had hoped, that invisible spears and harpoons would pierce his sensitivities, that parts of his existence must be held down, that the things he would grow to find in himself were the very things he should drive away, that many things he loved, he could surely find, but never keep. He had met again that small Theodore who was crawling through it all, who was wading and reeling along every destructive force, and now he was holding onto the feeling, holding onto himself, taking notice of the distance and the change through time from then till now.

It came upon him like a fallen cloth—that state of thought that veils the eyes and wakes the amorphous field of memory that is held down by emotion. Shaken out of a long slumber, it poured into reality, devouring it as a mirror devours the shapes, the lights, the shadows of a room, creating the vanishing point of space. It was the spacing out into chambers of unreality, where residues of his life, of days and months and years, converged and created a single point of concentration. It was the dim re-living of what formed the story of his past, his awareness lightly grazing upon times of joy, of despair, of wonder, of humour, of finding, in days, nights, alone, with friends, lovers, parents, siblings, teachers, those he admired, those he wished to know, those who hurt him, those who made him afraid, who helped him, whom he helped, in places he loved, despised, wished to return, in times he hoped to keep—each a thread in the fabric that made him. The song began to grow, to slide upwards, and quite suddenly, similar to a whistle that bleeds into the middle of night, it had him on the glide of its venture, where he noticed the precise way it was moving. It was in fact going nowhere in particular, but its potentiality was everywhere, impossible to predict. Each second comprised nothing but the unnoticed, those unconscious sensations sent to and brought out by the perceiver of the moment, too fleeting to capture, too slight to fathom. Here, he had discovered something new, he had bitten into the fabric that no longer evaded him. The song behind the hands pressed the body of the piano with no methodology, this abundant way of letting it out, lending the notes a dazzle, a brightness, a sadness, then a twinkle of humour, then a question, and a wondering, then a realisation, a pause, a conglomerate that was quiet, sustained, then big, fine like the mark of a pencil, then wide and deep as a spout in the sky, then steady as a pool that would remain unchanged, before it poured once more, then found a rhythm, a rhythm that was cloaked in a quiet neutrality, and feeling, a back and forth like an eternal pendulum, a sinking and a rising, and again a rhythm, before it broke into slower moments, and the floating tune began to sink, deep—deeper. And this state that Theodore had come to think about, this whole and unsullied way of being that was marked in the song, how vague but familiar it was to him; he recognised it like a thing he had at times known and at other times became a stranger to, never quite truly noticing its soundless slipping away. But what mattered was that he had known it, that it could be found somewhere inside of him. It had subsumed him that night he reunited with Yvonne, for his words then were spilling out of him in bursts of effortless insight; it had produced the very thing he had told her about that night, that final note cast by the glide along the cello, when he had become suddenly aware of its blinding vanishing; he had known it often in his early years of life, before he had built a circuity around it as he learned to mould his mind, to calculate his actions, to slit with harsh judgement his own findings of love, his cares, his affections; it was what inspired the impulse of his hand to hold another, and what he sought in the room full of books under the staircase in his family home when his yearning had led him to wonder in the solitude of night. And it was what came over him the moment he stuck his fingers into the clay and set out to find what he could make. That world of clay that soon became Gaius was the opportunity to let his hands re-ignite it, to work with the mind of his authenticity, his imperishable fondness. And he had let them do just that. He had made the simulacrum of the feeling. He had ventured to let what is beautiful come to fruition. That feeling, he came to realise, was the thing he cherished so dearly, so it was no surprise to him now that he had given Gaius an imagined sentience, that he had formed a care for the sculpture much greater than any care he had given to any other inanimate object. He realised something that rose out of nothing at all: that, that right there, is what Gaius is. Gaius is the moment's call. Gaius is the awareness that wonders without the weight of burden, that invents without scarcity, that is nourished by the seeds of connection, that finds goodness without division—that feels, and so does.

The steam was now a molten shape as he watched it through a lens wetted with heavy tears that resisted falling. He came back to himself, to the song that was now growing lighter, higher. He drank the tea as it faded, until it reached nothing, a static silence followed by a click that marked the end of the recording. Cadeo opened his eyes, blinking as he adjusted to the light. Something about the sweet silence that now filled the room felt to be the most appropriate response. It was the slow windy sigh that streams across the faces of saplings after a spectacle in a gloaming sky. A howl in response to blessed light. And so light was the air between them, the startling fantasy of a pure and earthly passion. Out from the passage of forgotten time, he smiled to Cadeo, who smiled back.

— Thank you, whispered Theodore.

And then he left, quietly, feeling that was all he now needed to do, to leave, to return.

He travelled through his return with care to notice: the grassy hills, the hedges, the thrushes, the paths that swivelled like a hummingbird, the terracotta walls on the adjoining homes, the carrying of the train, the windows that were revealing mists along the landscapes and beneath the evergreens and structures of stone. There, in the steadiness of piercing through the breeze within the tilting cradle of the carriage, he noticed that the breath passing through him was like that of a novel creature, one that lives without the gnarled blades that impale and hook at the arrival of a dark place, or the after-clap of lightning that strikes the root of a sacred plant. He discovered in him a primitive sense that preceded the blemish, or the flaw that held him from the jump, the glide, the soar into high peaks. The unlearning to be bound—the realisation of the albatross who once learned its wings are needless props.

After heading out of the train station, he decided to walk along the pathway of a park he adored, to catch the last hints of light before the evening would take place. A pergola under which he walked, with trailing vines that captured surprises of blue, appeared to be an entranceway that bordered a place where things grew from the radicles of grace. It was no longer the park through which he had walked perhaps a hundred times, but a place where things were alive in many ways and contortions, some this, some that, all with the opportunity to change, to sprout in another direction, to allow shapes to form within them. Nothing was curtailed, all was, in relation to one another, taking part in the pattern in the impulse of the instant. The abandoned picnic blanket in the branches was like a sylph, sent happily to twirl among the call of the birds, one of them the ring-necked pheasant, whose red face and mottled wings moved in and out of the thickets as it pleased. There was something about its call, as it was fused with the sharp recollection of the piano melody that had filled the exit of Cadeo's home, and the flaring rays of sunset that were poking out from bodies of chalk-dust now and then, that produced in him a sensation whose touch he could only obscurely recall; it was perhaps an existential joy, a sense of all things perceived culminating into one visceral language. A knowing that, despite him and his delicate human vessel, the very thing that made him entirely here, the quake that caused him to be alive, was indeed indestructible. It was the feeling he searched for in his younger years after it had been taken from him, at times reaching the threshold of it, never quite being the subject of its complete face. Oftentimes he had thought of himself standing against the backdrop of everything around him, and suddenly the backdrop became the entire world, and then there would be him and his minuscule mind, kept tight and enclosed because of fear to allow it to expand, that something was holding it back, and in these moments it seemed that to discover the world was a menacing thing. But in this spread-out junction of before and after, to discover the world was in fact the most natural thing, the impulse written in every touch of his fingertips, each look of his eyes. He felt that his words and his mannerisms would create patterns in the air, that any endeavour he would embark on, big or small, would trace hills of adventure. And he felt that when the ambience would change and sadness would inevitably find him again, at least it would be tinged with the remnant of this very knowing. Tones of early darkness came to mark its presence, and right where the night bled on the sky, he got a sense, as if plucking it out from where it had been lodged, that he was now skimming the edge of lack. The lack that was once like a bite one could never recover from, and that had once bitten him. But it could no longer be a riddle with no start or end, a lock whose shape required an impossible key, for it was no longer him. And to despise it? Here, he wished not even to do that. For a wind does not stand still to scorn the wall that obstructs it, it simply keeps on.

Somewhere among finding small pieces along the path— the grass, the butterfly that perforated the sunlight, the blue kite, the person over there whose hands were lost in weaving the looms, the one laughing by the bluebells, the one capturing the trees with a camera—he heard a hoot come from behind him. And then his name, out from the spirited voice of Yvonne. He turned around, and through the wetness of his tear-stained pupils, he saw her running towards him, her shapeless clothes igniting the hollow, jumping loaves of bread in the basket over her shoulder. She stood in front of him, catching her breath. And it was right there, in that particular light caught in the point where their sights met, the light that was somehow visible and unseen, ancient and young, earthly and astral, he observed a quiet throb run through the insides of him that was like a lightning urge to tell. Because what he would tell, she would understand. It was abundant, and he knew it was, and he could not tell how he knew it, because abundance cannot quantify itself, it can only let what's coming come, and set free what wishes to run. It was a fine tuning of knowing that she, among other things he had found and would find, was a place that would nurture and sow the soils of his world, that here, all of him could belong, in every shape and sound he might become. And that belonging was recognised now that they were laying in one another's eyes, wishing to care, finding traces of themselves where wishes gently knock before they bloom. So slight but so real the idea was, the idea that maybe, with persistence, he could speak the unspeakable, that together they could find that place where all that was pure could be given attention. And they would never run dry, because this was the thread of the greatness of being, of communication, of imparting, of play, and it was limitless because it was existence. Pulling him out of his stricken silence of thought, she ruffled her nose, and with a knowing look and a laugh that indicated an eagerness to find, she spoke:

— Tell me.

When he knocked on the door, a small fidget that was the avidity of two weeks advanced in his knuckle. Soon, the unlocking bolt sounded, then the door wafted open, the air of the hallway and the home marrying right where he stood. Standing there was Himari and her absorbing self, her stiff but somehow fluid stature, smudges of sapphire blue across her cheeks and her cupid's bow. She greeted him and keenly let him in, and just like before, that same sweet scent of scattered pungency found in all of earth's corners massed together and floated towards him.

— I've been eager to finally show the sculpture to you, she said as she led him through the hallway.

The cat, in pristine motion, jumped from a table and walked along by, sliding its fur across his ankles, seemingly acknowledging his arrival before disappearing into another room. He walked behind Himari into the living room. When he followed the line of her pointing finger leading him to a spot above the mantlepiece, he gasped a flamed breath at what he saw: there, Gaius stood, rebuilt and entire, beckoning poise and enchantment with nothing but a silent arrangement of parts, engraved with new patterns of gold, so inimitable and animate that it was quite unbelievable that they hadn't always been there. The whole of it had been restored to a form that was even bolder, brighter. He stepped forward to see the sculpture closely. Golden lines were set as bending roads where lashes of other passages came, like a river of a thousand amulets, laid with care and precision by hands with a stillness summoned from far beneath the ground. It was a fine surprise that the gold cloaked the entirety of it with something so extraordinary, a raw mineral extracted from the cores of the most intimate caves, held beneath fire to melt and fall as tears that would stain and leave behind solid traces. The air in the room filled with intrigue. After clearing her throat, Himari spoke:

— You want to know something? Gaius was one of my favourite pieces to mend. After you left him with me I began to adore his broken character. I took time with him. I waited for the precise moment of each day to put his pieces together, which happened to be when the sky was at its most vibrant and layered. He's ready now. You can take him.

Theodore took a step back, not once looking away from the sculpture. So profound it was to see it in its entirety again, like this. He wondered how a clod of clay, a little piece of moist fine-grained earth had lain in his palm, had sat there lifelessly, and all at once had been nothing but what it wasn't, extracted like a nettle's hair wedged into the pore of a finger, taken from its own limitation to merge and become what it was now. And who would have thought that it would have come to be this way, that it would have ended up here?

— You've done something really special with him.

— What is special was there before I began, replied Himari. I must tell you something. Last night, after I had finished putting the final pieces together, I sat by and looked at him right there where he is. Some small piece of light from the moon came into the room, lit him up. Then everything was so still. I stayed and watched him for a while, cloaked in the light. After some time, from where I sat it looked almost like the gold I had placed between the parts was coming from inside of the clay, like it had filled the inner surfaces and all the entrails and was now overflowing, bursting through, spilling out of the cracks. Looking at it in that way, something came to mind: Gaius suddenly became the subject of a story I want to tell. You see, I haven't been able to encounter the glint of an idea that I've been wishing to find; I've been starting things and leaving them in half-written fragments, unmoved by the contents. But since I finished with him, I haven't quite been able to take my hand away from the pen.

On the table beside her, Theodore observed scattered papers in patterns of all sorts, stacked with lines of fine and angular writings, scribblings that gathered to the end of the pages, and drawings of Gaius among vortexes of ink and words. Everything spilt across the tabletop like hands seeping into applause. Then he turned his focus to cross the vibrant walls, and looked all around.

— I think the best place for Gaius is right there, up here in this home with you.

— No, said Himari, sharply. I don't wish to take him from you.

— Please, keep him, he said quietly and with a mark of kind finality, smiling at her now. But, Himari, will you do one thing, and that is when your story is complete, will you read it to me?

Out of a hushed breath, Himari nodded, and then sat down and held her hands together in a circular hold, while her face became full in colour, and somewhere in it, he saw a transparent pleasure that was rare to come by, the kind of look in the face of a watchful child as a leaf of treasured appearances falls to lay in their hands. And with that being the final thing, he said goodbye, leaving her settled in the chair. Then, stepping through the dim corridor towards the door, something on the wall roused his attention. A painting, of parts that shadows could not contain. He turned on the light and saw before him a medley of earthly pigments, the parts and dimensions overlapping, altogether gleaming. The patterns were so obscure and plentiful that he could have seen many things, but what he saw now, viewed up close, was the shape of a small organ, perhaps a heart, its surface reflecting light like porcelain, and this heart was wrapped in arms of bending branches, leafless, but on the hands were many furrows like folding petals in heavy winds, floating, crepuscular, vibrating in sound so their outlines were waved and winding. And framing it all were circles of misty orbs, a thousand eyes blinking on the surface of an astral glow, merging into one route. A membrane of slow beauty. But when he stepped back against the wall behind and looked again, all that he saw had vanished, wiped out to the very last remain, and what his sight drew now was something simpler, incomprehensible, a thing that touched the heart's pulse. It was aliveness, dwelling in the tinted movement of a hand that swayed to the telling of what was unboundedly whole.

And on the low corner a curling name was marked in faint whitish yellow: Cadeo. Down the wall he noticed more of the paintings that he had somehow overlooked. And he could have stayed there for a long time and looked at them all if it wasn't for the urge to go out into the nightly air, and the knowing that eventually he'd be back. Once more, he called goodbye, and then he left. He went down the stairs, and outside, where he could feel the roar and hear the hum of a night in easy luminescence. He turned around, looked up, first to the window where the small flutter of a candle drew a gentle pulse on the pane, where Yvonne sat nearby, expecting his arrival, absorbed in the happenings in the distance. Then he looked to the window above, where his tilting gaze once more found the small stature of Gaius, a novel piece standing amongst a world of many sorts and things, of inestimable sentiments and pleasures, like starlight that has fallen into the atmosphere. Seen from afar, the impact of its presence still resounded, still etched a hearty impression. From up there, it let free a measureless word that reached below and touched him in a thread of bonded thoughts: that he would seek to craft his fortune, that from his field of mind he would unhook the ends of his parameters, that he would remember to hold out his hand, to himself, to another, and with it say yes to the endless good that is found in becoming and belonging, that he would let himself imagine, that he would throw himself into all that he loved. Entirely awake, he perceived the moment as a mystery, composed in every hue and shade imaginable, an expanse of soft grounds from where anything could flourish. So, leaving not a remnant of doubt behind, he went into it.

Printed in Great Britain
by Amazon